I0726956

31 DAYS OF

speaking

LIFE

CONFESSIONS FOR HEALTHY RELATIONSHIP

THE RELATIONSHIP DRS.

DRS. TIMOTHY & MONIQUE JOHNS

31 Days of Speaking Life

Confessions for Healthy Relationships

By The Relationship Drs./Drs. Timothy & Monique Johns

Cover & Logo Designed by Louisa P. Handy

Published by Jazzy Kitty Publications

Editor: Anelda L. Attaway

Co-editor: Monique Johns

© 2023 Timothy Johns

ISBN 978-1-954425-75-0

Library of Congress Control Number: 2023905847

DEDICATION

Mom & Dad, Thank you for listening and being our mediator for 27 years. Your consistent example has prevailed/pushed us to continue to pursue a deeper relationship with God. Thank you for holding us accountable to our vows.

To our grandparents of 110 years, Harvey & Cassie Brown, and Jonas & Elizabeth Ford, for their demonstration of commitment, loyalty, and LOVE for family. When we lose Grace on any given day, we remember the LOVE you portrayed and presented, and we recognize how Blessed we really are to have each other. HONOR & LOVE

To our Spiritual Parents who have poured the experience and wisdom into us, we thank you!

TABLE OF CONTENTS

<h1 style="text-align:center">TABLE OF CONTENTS</h1>

TABLE OF CONTENTS

INTRODUCTION

This is 31 days of confession, a daily renewal for the heart, mind, and soul.

Daily Renewal

I commit myself to this daily that
I will honor and love you unconditionally.

Day One Destined to Rule ~ We have Dominion.

1. We Decree and Declare that we are Destined to Rule together.

2. We Decree and Declare Dominion over our household.

3. We Decree and Declare our children are Blessed.

4. We Decree and Declare we are unified, and we always walk in agreement.

5. We Decree and Declare NO weapon formed against us shall prosper.

6. We Decree and Declare we ALWAYS are led by the Spirit, and we take possession of our inheritance.

7. We Decree and Declare our tongues are like a pin of a ready writer, and we speak life always.

8. We Decree and Declare we ALWAYS speak the truth in LOVE under the Power of Grace.

9. We Decree and Declare that all things are possible for us because we believe God.

10. We Decree and Declare God is our shield and protector.

11. We Decree and Declare that we walk in unconditional honor and unconditional love.

12. We Decree and Declare the Favor of God is increasing in our lives daily.

13. We Decree and Declare, we call those things that be not as though they were, and with our eyes, we see them come to pass.

14. We Decree and Declare that the Heavens belong to God, but He has given the earth to us to rule and reign.

15. We Decree and Declare that our Word will never return to us void, but it will accomplish everything we send it to do in Jesus' Name.

16. We Decree and Declare our Faith in God's words has made us an overcomer.

17. We Decree and Declare, we believe therefore, we speak what we hear in the secret place and we see those things come to pass.

18. We Decree and Declare this our time to Prosper in every area of our Lives, Marriage, Family, Career, Ministry and Finances in Jesus' Name.

19. We Decree and Declare that our voice strengthens our angelic support.

20. We Decree and Declare we command our ministering spirits to be loosed now to perform the Word of God spoken over our Marriage, Family, Career, Ministry, and Finances in Jesus' Name.

21. We Decree and Declare that angels are responding this day to bring to past everything spoken in this confession in Jesus' Name.

22. We Decree and Declare that we are more than conquers in Jesus' Name.

23. We Decree and Declare we will always triumph in Christ Jesus.

24. We Decree and Declare God will be done, and His kingdom come now in Jesus' Name.

25. We Decree and Declare we will dwell in Your house Forever and Forever.

Then God said, "Let Us make man in Our image,

according to Our likeness; let them have dominion.

Genesis 2:26 (NKJV)

Reflections

Day Two ~ Knowing who you are

1. We Decree and Declare we are the Righteousness of God.

2. We Decree and Declare that NO weapon formed against us shall prosper.

3. We Decree and Declare that we are Faithful to the Relationship/ Marriage.

4. We Decree and Declare we are Dedicated to our Relationship/ Marriage.

5. We Decree and Declare we are Dedicated to our Relationship/ Marriage.

6. We Decree and Declare we are the Love of God.

7. We Decree and Declare as Jesus is; so are we in this world.

8. We Decree and Declare we are the Redeemed of God.

9. We Decree and Declare we are the Fruit of God.

10. We Decree and Declare we are the BLESSED of God.

11. We Decree and Declare that our relationship/marriage is abounding for every good work.

12. We Decree and Declare our Relationship/Marriage is strong and courageous.

13. We Decree and Declare that our relationship/marriage will overcome every obstacle and setbacks.

14. We Decree and Declare our relationship/marriage reflects God in the earth.

15. We Decree and Declare our relationship/marriage is healed from

all wounds in our soul in Jesus' Name.

16. We Decree and Declare we are God's masterpiece.

17. We Decree and Declare we are Beloved of God.

18. We Decree and Declare we believe; therefore, we speak; all things work for our relationship.

19. Relationship/Marriage is a SUCCESS.

20. We Decree and Declare our relationship/marriage reflects the Favor of God.

21. We Decree and Declare our Relationship/Marriage is Strengthened by the Word of God.

22. We Decree and Declare our Relationship/Marriage is Upheld by God.

23. We Decree and Declare our Relationship/Marriage is Sustained by God.

24. We Decree and Declare our Relationship/Marriage is Perfected by God.

25. We Decree and Declare we are One in Christ Jesus.

The Consummation of Love

Love has been perfected among us in this: that we may have boldness in the day of judgment; because as He is, so are we in this world.

1 John 4:17 (NKJV)

Reflections

Day Three ~ Enlarge Our Territory

1. We Decree and Declare we WILL INCREASE MORE AND MORE, even our Children.
2. We Decree and Declare and the Lord loads us up daily with benefits.
3. We Decree and Declare that we increase in knowledge.
4. We Decree and Declare that we increase in wisdom.
5. We Decree and Declare that we increase in understanding.
6. We Decree and Declare all Grace abounds in us for every good work.
7. We Decree and Declare we multiply and are fruitful in every endeavor unto the Lord.
8. We Decree and Declare the Blessings of the Lord have overtaken us as we obey the Lord.
9. We Decree and Declare we Prosper in the things of God and everything we touch is Blessed.
10. We Decree and Declare that our territory is enlarging daily.
11. We Decree and Declare our daily lives reflect the Favor of God.
12. We Decree and Declare the Favor of God rests on my MINISTRY.
13. We Decree and Declare the Favor of God rests on our children.
14. We Decree and Declare the Favor of God increases in our lives.
15. We Decree and Declare the Favor of God causes our relationship to experience preferential treatment.
16. We Decree and Declare the Favor of God causes us to experience new opportunities daily.
17. We Decree and Declare we reign in righteousness and justice.
18. We Decree and Declare today that we will experience life abundantly.

19. We Decree and Declare we ALWAYS experience the Favor of God.

20. We Decree and Declare we flow in the Grace of God, and supernatural increase is our portion.

21. We Decree and Declare we thank God for giving us everything pertaining to Life and Godliness.

22. We Decree and Declare that we receive and take possession of every promise the Word of God said about Marriage, Family, Ministry, Finances and Career in Jesus' Name.

23. We Decree and Declare poverty, lack, and insufficiency is a curse in Jesus' Name.

24. We Decree and Declare that we call every good thing to come to us now in Jesus' Name.

25. We Decree and Declare the Blessings of the Lord have made us rich with no sorrow.

*And Jabez called on the God of Israel saying, "Oh, that You would bless me indeed, and enlarge my [a]territory, that Your hand would be with me, and that You would keep *me* from evil, that I may not cause pain!" So, God granted him what he requested.

1 Chronicles 4:10

Reflections

Day Four ~ Growing in Grace

1. We Decree and Declare that we Grow in Knowledge.

2. We Decree and Declare that we Multiply in the Knowledge of God.

3. We Decree and Declare that we Grow in the Grace of God.

4. We Decree and Declare that the Grace of God surrounds us everywhere we go.

5. We Decree and Declare the Grace of God covers up, like eagles' wings.

6. We Decree and Declare that the Grace of God protects us.

7. We Decree and Declare the Grace of God goes before us.

8. We Decree and Declare the Grace of God has established us in our place of destiny.

9. We Decree and Declare the Grace of God covers our mistakes with goodness and mercy.

10. We Decree and Declare the Grace of God helps us resist temptation.

11. We Decree and Declare the Grace of God gives us Favor with our enemies.

12. We Decree and Declare the Grace of God gives us the power to stand during challenging times and seasons.

13. We Decree and Declare the Grace of God gives us supernatural results in all our endeavors.

14. We Decree and Declare the Grace of God is the Power of God, brings us into experiencing the benefits of the Cross.

15. We Decree and Declare that the Grace of God has healed our bodies, and we walk in divine healing daily.

16. We Decree and Declare that the Grace of God protects us from every virus and disease.

17. We Decree and Declare that the Grace of God gives us the legal right to prosper in every area of our lives.

18. We Decree and Declare that the Grace of God goes before us and makes all the crooked places straight.

19. We Decree and Declare that the Grace of God established our names in the Lamb Book of Life.

20. We Decree and Declare that the Grace of God empowers us to overcome every demonic attack against our Marriage, Family, Ministry, Career and Finances in Jesus' Name.

21. We Decree and Declare that the Word of Grace has given us divine strategies to win and dominate in this earthly realm.

22. We Decree and Declare that the Word of Grace always warns us of danger, and we will never stumble in Jesus' Name.

23. We Decree and Declare it is God's Grace that restores everything that was lost or stolen from us, in Jesus' Name.

24. We Decree and Declare that the Grace of God takes us from Faith to Faith and Glory to Glory.

25. We Decree and Declare the Grace of God enables us to finish strong.

God planned long ago to choose you by making you His holy people, which is the Spirit's work. God wanted you to obey Him and to obey Him and to be made clean by the blood of the death of Jesus Christ.

Grace and peace be yours more and more.

1 Peter 1 2-3

Reflections

Day Five ~ Overcoming Disappointment

1. We Decree and Declare we are overcomers by blood and our testimony.

2. We Decree and Declare what the enemy meant for evil; God is working out for our good.

3. We Decree and Declare that as we sow in tears, we shall reap in joy.

4. We Decree and Declare our strength is made perfect in our weakness.

5. We Decree and Declare that NO weapon formed against us shall prosper.

6. We Decree and Declare we are ALWAYS led by the Spirit and not by our flesh.

7. We Decree and Declare that the Lord is our Shepherd, and we shall not want.

8. We Decree and Declare our emotions towards one another are healthy and Spirit led.

9. We Decree and Declare that we always walk in Grace toward one another.

10. We Decree and Declare we walk in unconditional honor toward one another.

11. We Decree and Declare that we always speak the truth mixed with Grace.

12. We Decree and Declare we never get frustrated with one another as we press towards the mark.

13. We Decree and Declare that we always speak the truth mixed with Grace.

14. We Decree and Declare when we can't take it anymore; we willingly die to our flesh and hit the reset button.

15. We Decree and Declare our relationship will reflect the Image of God.

16. We Decree and Declare my mate will meet all my needs.

17. We Decree and Declare that we see each other through the Lens of God.

18. We Decree and Declare we always forgive.

19. We Decree and Declare we will never quit.

20. We Decree and Declare that we will never give up.

21. We Decree and Declare we will never settle for less than what God has for our Relationship/Marriage.

22. We Decree and Declare that we will never settle for less than what God has for our Relationship/Marriage.

23. We Decree and Declare we will always encourage one another to be ALL that God has called us to be.

24. We Decree and Declare that we are more than conquers in Christ Jesus.

25. We will decree and declare that we will always encourage one another to be God's best.

And let us not grow weary while doing good, for in due season we shall reap

if we do not lose heart."

Galatians 6:9

Reflections

Day Six ~ Defeating the Giants

1. We Decree and Declare that the Lord is on our side; we shall fear no man.

2. We Decree and Declare we are in covenant with a Faithful God.

3. We Decree and Declare we release the Spirit of Praise against every demonic attack against our Marriage, Family, Ministry, Careers and Finances in Jesus' Name.

4. We Decree and Declare war against every spirit that would hinder or frustrate the plan of God for our lives.

5. We Decree and Declare we bind, pride, selfishness, envy, strife, and perversion in Jesus' Name.

6. We Decree and Declare we release humility, love, honor, peace, and purity in Jesus' Name.

7. We Decree and Declare this is the victory we have, and it is our Faith in our Lord Jesus Christ.

8. We Decree and Declare we Walk in the Spirit concerning one another and we will not fulfill the lust of our flesh.

9. We Decree and Declare that as for me and our house, we will serve the Lord.

10. We Decree and Declare Jesus is Lord over our entire household.

11. We Decree and Declare as Jesus is, so we are in this world.

12. We Decree and Declare we renounce selfishness, and we declare that Love rules in our house.

13. We Decree and Declare that the Love of God empowers us to always forgive and never be offended.

14. We Decree and Declare my husband/wife supplies all my needs.

15. We Decree and Declare I am fulfilled physically, emotionally, and intellectually from my husband/wife in Jesus' Name.

16. We Decree and Declare my husband/wife is my partner for life.

17. We Decree and Declare my love for my husband/wife anticipating their every need.

18. We Decree and Declare our steps are ordered by the Lord.

19. We Decree and Declare we are the righteousness of God in Christ Jesus.

20. We Decree and Declare we cancel every attack against our marriage/relationship in Jesus' Name.

21. We Decree and Declare; we release the light of the gospel into to every dark place in our marriage.

22. We Decree and Declare, let there be light in our marriage, let there be light in the lives of our children, let there be light in our finances, let there be light in our physical bodies and let there be light in our family in Jesus' Name.

23. We Decree and Declare that every financial need we have is met in Jesus' Name.

24. We Decree and Declare every tongue that raises up against us we will condemn in Jesus' Name.

25. We Decree and Declare that this battle is not ours, it is the Lord's.

"Then David put his hand in his bag and took out a stone; and he slung *it* and struck the Philistine in his forehead, so that the stone sank into his forehead and he fell on his face to the earth."

1 Samuel 17:49 (NKJV)

Reflections

Day Seven ~ Standing Alone

1. We Decree and Declare that today the Lord is on our side, and we will not fear while we are in a relationship.

2. We Decree and Declare today that the Lord is the light and our salvation in Jesus' Name.

3. We Decree and Declare today that the Lord is the strength of our relationship.

4. We Decree and Declare today that all things are possible for us with God.

5. We Decree and Declare today in our weakness; we are made strong to stand in every evil day.

6. We Decree and Declare today that wisdom is our armor bearer.

7. We Decree and Declare today in His presence that there is a fullness of Joy for our relationship.

8. We Decree and Declare today that the Lord is our Provider.

9. We Decree and Declare today that the Lord is our Shepherd.

10. We Decree and Declare today that the Lord is our Righteousness.

11. We Decree and Declare today the Lord is always there for us.

12. We Decree and Declare today that the Lord is our Sanctifier.

13. We Decree and Declare today that the Lord is our Banner.

14. We Decree and Declare today that the Lord is our Healer.

15. We Decree and Declare today that the Lord is our Protector.

16. We Decree and Declare today that the Lord is the Lord of breakthrough for us in our relationship.

17. We Decree and Declare today our strength is being renewed as we wait on God.

18. We shall soar like eagles and run and not get weary.

19. We Decree and Declare that today our faith will never fail concerning our relationship.

20. We Decree and Declare today that while we wait on the Lord we are being sanctified by His truth.

21. We Decree and Declare today that we have been chosen for such a time as this.

22. We Decree and Declare today that before the foundation of the world, our relationship was chosen by God in Christ Jesus.

23. We Decree and Declare today what the devil has meant for evil; God has turned around for our good.

24. We Decree and Declare today that a cycle has been completed and old things have passed away and all things have been made new. Tomorrow we will step into a new day.

25. We Decree and Declare today that the Lord is our Expectation.

"This I Declare, about the Lord: He alone is my refuge,

my place of safety; he is my God, and I trust him"

Psalms 91:2 (NLT)

Reflections

Day Eight – Overcoming Temptation

1. We decree and declare that no weapon formed against our relationship shall prosper

2. We condemn and cancel every attack against our marriage, family, and children

3. We put on the whole armor of God

4. The shield of faith protects us from every fair dart of the enemy

5. We decree and declare we walk in the Spirit and will not fulfill the lust of the flesh

6. As we watch and pray, we hear the voice of God, and the voice of the enemy will not follow

7. The weapons of our warfare are not carnal but mighty for pulling down every stronghold

8. We dwell in the secret place of the highest and abide in the shadow of the almighty

9. The Lord is our refuge and hiding place

10. No evil shall fall on us and no plague shall come near our dwelling

11. We resist the devil, and he shall flee

12. We stand in the grace of God, and we have access to God's supernatural power

13. We are more than a conqueror in Christ Jesus

14. We always triumph in Christ and our victory is guaranteed by the blood of Jesus

15. We plead the blood over our entire household, our children, our possession, and our finances

16. Weeping may endure for a night, but joy has come to our house this morning

17. We decree and declare this is the day that Lord has made, and we shall rejoice

18. We decree and declare that angles are encamped around, protecting us from dangers seen and unseen.

19. We bind the spirit of pride, selfishness, and lust and we loose the love of God in our relationship

20. We decree and declare that we always walk in love and the enemy has no access to our lives

21. As we walk in love we will never be offended, and we will always forgive each other

22. We decree and declare we will not be moved by what we see, we are only moved by what God has said

23. The Holy Spirit is our guide and comforter

24. We walk in the will of God in every area of our life and his truth is our shield and buckler

25. We decree and declare that the devil is defeated, and he is under our feet in Jesus' Name

"Then He said to them, "Why do you sleep?

Rise and pray, lest you enter temptation."

Luke 22:46 (NKJV)

Reflections

Day Nine ~ Hungry for More

1. We Decree and Declare today that the Blessing of the Lord has made us rich with no sorrow.

2. We Decree and Declare today some plants and some waters, but God has given us an increase.

3. We Decree and Declare today an increase in our homes.

4. We Decree and Declare today an increase in our jobs, careers, and businesses.

5. We Decree and Declare today an increase in the lives of our children.

6. We Decree and Declare today that as we hunger and thirst, we shall be filled.

7. We Decree and Declare today that our Love of God causes us to prosper on a daily basis.

8. We Decree and Declare today that out of the fruit of our mouths, our innermost desires will be filled.

9. We Decree and Declare that today we will not allow any corrupt word to proceed out of our mouths, only that which is edifying to those who hear it.

10. We Decree and Declare today that we bind Lack, Insufficiency and Poverty and lose abundance in the Name of Jesus.

11. We Decree and Declare today all things work out for our Good.

12. We Decree and Declare today; that we are loaded up daily with God's benefits.

13. We are always abounding in the Work of the Lord.

14. We Decree and Declare today that our relationship gives off a reflection that reveals God in the earth.

15. We Decree and Declare today, we increase daily in the Wisdom of God and Understanding.

16. We Decree and Declare today our relationship is rooted and grounded in Love.

17. We Decree and Declare today that we received the fruits of our Labor of Love.

18. We Decree and Declare today that Prosperity is ours, Healing is ours, and Deliverance is ours in Jesus' Name.

19. We Decree and Declare today that we received every good thing from our Father in Heaven.

20. We Decree and Declare today we reject everything that God is not in.

21. We Decree and Declare today that we Honor the Lord with all that we have and we are content with our portion.

22. We Decree and Declare today that we Thank You, Lord, for all things pertaining to life and Godliness.

23. We Decree and Declare today that we Thank You, Lord, for Your goodness and mercy.

24. We Decree and Declare today we Thank You, Lord, that we have abundance because of the cross.

25. We Decree and Declare today that we will dwell in Your house Forever and Forever.

The Lord shall increase you more and more, you and your children.

Ye are blessed of the Lord which made heaven and earth. The heaven, even the heavens, are the Lord's: but the earth hath he given to the children of men."

Psalm 115:14-16 (KJV)

Reflections

Day Ten ~ Dynamic Faith

1. We Decree and Declare today in the Name of Jesus; I am a believer.

2. We Decree and Declare today that I believe God's Word.

3. We Decree and Declare today I am what the Word says I am.

4. We Decree and Declare today. I have what the Word says I have.

5. We Decree and Declare today I can do what the Word says I can do.

6. I render ineffective every negative word against my life and marriage.

7. We Decree and Declare today every word was spoken that is a contradiction to the Will of God; I curse in the Name of Jesus.

8. We Decree and Declare today from this moment forward, I will acknowledge on the good things that are in me in Christ Jesus.

9. We Decree and Declare today that out of the good treasures of my heart only good things will come to pass.

10. We Decree and Declare today I am the Righteousness of God; I am a new creation; I am a joint heir with Jesus.

11. We Decree and Declare today I have been delivered from the power of darkness and translated into the Kingdom of God.

12. We Decree and Declare today that I have been redeemed by the Blood of the Lamb, redeemed from the Curse, redeemed from Sickness, Disease, Poverty, and Death.

13. We Decree and Declare today we can do all things through Christ who strengthens us.

14. We are more than conquerors.

15. We Decree and Declare today that He never leaves us or forsakes us.

16. We Decree and Declare today since the Greater One dwells in us, we can overcome every situation.

17. We Decree and Declare today that the Faith of God resides in us and through it, we have the victory that has overcome the world.

18. We Decree and Declare today that I Thank You, Father that we can do all things.

19. We Decree and Declare today that we believe in our hearts and have released it with our mouths, and it will surely come to pass in Jesus' Name.

20. We Decree and Declare today we call things that be not, as though they were and release our Faith for supernatural results.

21. We Decree and Declare today that we are experiencing a supernatural acceleration in every area of our lives.

22. We Decree and Declare today our relationship with our spouse/partner is growing to the Glory of God.

23. We Decree and Declare today that our relationship with our God is growing daily.

24. We Decree and Declare today that our relationship with our children is growing to the Glory of God.

25. We Decree and Declare today that the Grace of God is upon me, enabling me to accomplish every word spoken this day in Jesus' Name.

For whatever is born of God overcomes the world. And this is the victory that has overcome the world—our faith.

1 John 5:4 (NKJV)

Reflections

Day Eleven ~ Having the Right Attitude

1. We Decree and Declare today that we have the right attitude; our minds are set on the things above.

2. We Decree and Declare today that we will think ourselves happy concerning our relationship.

3. We Decree and Declare today we always have the right attitude in every situation, every circumstance, and every hindrance.

4. We Decree and Declare today, Father, we Thank You that the communication of our Faith is made effectual by us acknowledging every good thing in Christ Jesus.

5. We Decree and Declare today that we hear the Voice of the Shepherd and the voice of a stranger we will not follow.

6. We Decree and Declare today Father, we believe You with our heart, and we say with our mouths that this day You will be done in our relationship.

7. We Decree and Declare today that we walk in a way worthy of a manner that pleases You and we desire to please You in all things.

8. We Decree and Declare today that our marriage is bearing fruit in every good work.

9. We Decree and Declare today that Jesus has been made Wisdom for us.

10. We are singularly minded; we walk in the Wisdom of God and expect to be on top in every situation.

11. We Decree and Declare today our minds are set, and our emotions are stable and grounded in the Word of God.

12. We Decree and Declare today that we desire to do Your Work, and our thoughts are aggregable to Your Will.

13. We Decree and Declare today that our plans are established in Your Word and we will succeed.

14. We Decree and Declare today that our steps are ordered and You make them sure.

15. We Decree and Declare today that we understand and firmly grasp what the Will of God is for our relationship; it's not vague, thoughtless, or foolish.

16. We Decree and Declare today we stand firm, grow spiritually mature and are fully convinced that Your Word is true.

17. We Decree and Declare today we are destined and appointed to progressively know You, to perceive and to recognize and become better and more intimately acquainted with Your Will for our lives.

18. We Decree and Declare today that the Holy Spirit abides in us permanently and guides us into all truth.

19. We are sanctified by the truth.

20. We Decree and Declare today that our thought is like a pen of a writer, and we only speak what God has said.

21. We Decree and Declare today we announce and declare Your Will to be manifested today in our thinking.

22. We Decree and Declare today as we think so were.

23. We Decree and Declare that today we have the Mind of Christ, the Thoughts of Christ, the Feelings of Christ, and the Purposes of Christ in our hearts and in our relationships.

24. We Decree and Declare today we think ourselves happy.

25. We Decree and Declare that today we have entered the Blessed rest by adhering, trusting, and relying on You.

"I think myself happy, King Agrippa, because today I shall answer for myself before you concerning all the things of which I am accused by the Jews"

Acts 26:2 (NKJV)

Reflections

Day Twelve ~ Forgiveness

1. We Decree and Declare that today old things have passed away; all things have been made new.

2. We Decree and Declare today that we are free from all the emotional pain of our past.

3. We Decree and Declare today we forgive those who trespass against us, and we receive the Lord's forgiveness for any wrong we have committed.

4. We Decree and Declare today that we repent from all wrong thinking concerning our relationships.

5. We Decree and Declare today that we renounce every idle word spoken in our relationships.

6. We close every demonic door that we have given to the enemy with our words.

7. We Decree and Declare today, and we command every spirit that is not like You to leave our relationship now in the Name of Jesus.

8. We Decree and Declare today that we cancel every attack against us, and we enforce the Will of God today in Jesus.

9. We Decree and Declare today we superimpose the Will of God concerning our relationship over the will of Satan in Jesus.

10. We Decree and Declare today that we will always walk in love and never receive an offense.

11. We Decree and Declare today we plead the Blood of Jesus on an emotional wound.

12. We Decree and Declare today that we speak to our soul, "Be healed in Jesus' Name."

13. We Decree and Declare today we speak to our heart, "Be healed in Jesus' Name."

14. We speak to our mind, "Be healed in Jesus' Name."

15. We Decree and Declare today we declare that everyone who has wronged us forgive and we call them Blessed in the Name of Jesus.

16. We Decree and Declare today every transgression against us forgiven and forgotten.

17. We Decree and Declare everything that has been held up because my sin be released now in Jesus' Name.

18. We Decree and Declare today that Restoration has come to our house.

19. We Decree and Declare today the Grace of God has enabled me to forgive, move forward, let go and think my self-happy concerning all who ever wronged me.

20. We Decree and Declare today I am a new creation in Christ Jesus.

21. We Decree and Declare today that my Love Walk is growing stronger by the day because I will always crucify my flesh.

22. We Decree and Declare today in our weakness, the Spirit of God has made me strong.

23. We Decree and Declare today, I am renewed in the spirit of my mind and the Joy of the Lord is my strength.

24. We Decree and Declare today. I abide in the Word and the Word abides in me, and I always experience a breakthrough.

25. We Decree and Declare today as greater is He, that he is in this world.

"And be kind to one another, tenderhearted, forgiving one another,

even as God in Christ forgave you."

Ephesians 4:32 (ESV)

Reflections

Day Thirteen ~ Unconditional Honor

1. We Decree and Declare today we walk in Unconditional Honor toward God and His Word.

2. We Decree and Declare Honor is a seed that gives me access to the Grace of God.

3. We Decree and Declare as we Honor God; God always honors us.

4. We Decree and Declare we daily offer Unconditional Honor to our spouse.

5. We Decree and Declare we Honor with our Words.

6. We Decree and Declare that we Honor them with our Bodies.

7. We Decree and Declare we Honor them with our Life.

8. We Decree and Declare we Honor them with our Love in Jesus' Name.

9. We Decree and Declare we understand that the Lack of Honor will produce failure, so we declare that the Word of God sets the boundaries for marriage/relationship, and we always experience great success.

10. We Decree and Declare in our marriage/relationship, we Honor the Words of Christ, and we receive His rewards.

11. We Decree and Declare that our marriage has been crowned with Glory and Honor.

12. We Decree and Declare our Honor towards God is producing supernatural increase, and because of Honor, we will never experience lack in our marriage.

13. We Decree and Declare our Marriage Reflects Honor.

14. We Decree and Declare our marriage is Established in Honor.

15. We Decree and Declare our marriage is Sustained by Honor.

16. We Decree and Declare that our marriage is Perfected by Honor.

17. We release a Spirit of Honor into our household.

18. We Decree and Declare our children will Walk in Honor.

19. We Decree and Declare because of Honor that Blessings flow to every area of our lives.

20. We Decree and Declare Honor flows in Ministry, Business, Marriage and in our Relationship.

21. We are the source of what Honor looks like.

22. We Decree and Declare Honor is the condition of our heart.

23. We Decree and Declare that every part of my soul Honors God (Mind, Will, Emotions, Imagination, and Thoughts).

24. We Decree and Declare we Honor our Father in all that we do.

25. We Decree and Declare we will Honor God in our marriage.

"...that each of you should know how to possess his own vessel

in sanctification and honor."

1 Thessalonians 4:4 (NKJV)

Reflections

Day Fourteen – Unconditional Love

1. We Decree and Declare that the Love of God has been shed in our hearts by the Holy Spirit because of the Love of God will never be hopeless.

2. We Decree and Declare because of the Love of God all the promises concerning us are Yes, and Amen to the Glory of God.

3. We Decree and Declare because of the Love of God, we will never fail.

4. We Decree and Declare the Love of God has united us, and we are one in Christ Jesus.

5. We Decree and Declare the Love of God has made us righteous.

6. We Decree and Declare that the Blessing of the Lord is on our head and flow to our entire household.

7. We Decree and Declare the Love of God has empowered us to always forgive.

8. We Decree and Declare our Love for one another is Unconditional and fills every gap in our relationship; our relationship lacks nothing is always abounding in the Grace of God.

9. We Decree and Declare that because of the Love of God we are more than conquerors in Christ Jesus.

10. We Decree and Declare that because of the Love of God we have dominion over the Works of God's hands.

11. We Decree and Declare that the Love of God has given us power over every negative circumstance, situation or contradiction that has affected our relationship.

12. We Decree and Declare because of the Love of God we never be

defeated, never separate, never divorce, and never stop growing in the Love of God.

13. We Decree and Declare that our Love for one another is growing daily, hourly, monthly, and yearly in Jesus' Name.

14. We Decree and Declare because of the Love of God we understand that our differences unite us and perfect us to the Glory of God.

15. We Decree and Declare that as God's Love is perfect so is our love for one another.

16. We Decree and Declare our Love for one another remove all fears in our relationship.

17. We Decree and Declare our love for one another, always anticipates the needs in my relationship.

18. We Decree and Declare the Love of God will always go the extra mile.

19. We Decree and Declare our Love for one another will never violate the boundaries of the Word of God.

20. We Decree and Declare our Love for one another is a choice and is not an emotional decision; we Choose to Love, we Walk in Love, we Live in Love, we Move in Love, and we have our being in love in Jesus' Name.

21. We Decree and Declare our Love for one another is selfless towards our relationship, towards our family and towards our neighbor and towards our friends.

22. We Decree and Declare because of the Love of God; our relationship will always abound with supernatural favor.

23. We Decree and Declare because of the Love of God; we are in possession of everything we need to have a successful relationship.

24. We Decree and Declare because of the Love of God; we will always produce Fruit of the Spirit. Love abounds in us, Joy abounds in us, Peace abounds in us, Kindness abounds in us, Faithfulness abounds in us, Goodness abounds in us, Longsuffering abounds in us, Gentleness abounds in us, and Self-control abounds in us.

25. We Decree and Declare our Love for one another is Unconditional.

And above all things, have fervent love for one another,

for love will cover a multitude of sins."

1 Peter 4:8 (NKJV)

Reflections

Day Fifteen ~ Commitment

1. We Decree and Declare we will NEVER leave or forsake our Relationship/Marriage.

2. We Decree and Declare we are Committed to honoring our covenant with God and our relationship.

3. We Decree and Declare that Honoring God above all else will be our focus and our delight.

4. We Decree and Declare that we are Committed to being a tree that is firmly planted in the Word of God.

5. We Decree and Declare we are Committed to never allowing our flesh and emotions to motivate outside the Will of God.

6. We Decree and Declare that we are Committed to believing that there is always Grace available in our times of weakness.

7. We Decree and Declare we are Committed to holding up a standard when the enemy comes in like a flood.

8. We are Committed to always speaking Life and not death.

9. We are Committed to seeking the Wisdom of God in every area of our Relationship, in our Finances, our Career, our Business, our Family, our Ministry.

10. We are Committed to fulfilling our divine assignment.

11. We are Committed to not allowing our differences to separate, destroy, or frustrate the Plan of God for our marriage.

12. We are Committed to being an example for other couples to follow.

13. We are Committed to going the extra mile concerning serving one another.

14. We are Committed to anticipating every need in our relationship and

doing everything possible to reflect the Love of God in our relationship.

15. We are Committed to dying to our flesh on a daily basis.

16. We are Committed to walking in Unconditional Honor, Unconditional Love, and the Grace of God.

17. We are Committed to growing in the Knowledge of God and seeking the Word of God to solve all our disagreements.

18. We are Committed to always agree concerning the things of God.

19. We are Committed to never allowing the enemy weapons to be used against us: strife, pride, arrogance, hate, and disdain.

20. We are Committed to never living in fear of one another.

21. We are Committed to having courage and boldness to always say what needs to be said in Love.

22. We are Committed to walking by Faith and not by sight.

23. We are Committed to never allowing our Faith to fail.

24. We are Committed to becoming a great listener.

25. We are Committed to a lifestyle of prayer concerning our relationship.

"For the Lord will not cast off His people,

nor will He forsake His inheritance."

Psalm 94:14 (NKJV)

Reflections

Day Sixteen ~ Covenant

1. We Decree and Declare we are the Righteousness of God in Christ Jesus.

2. We Decree and Declare we are in Covenant with God and co-laborers with Christ Jesus.

3. We Decree and Declare because of our Covenant with God, all the promises are Yes and Amen.

4. We Decree and Declare the promises are precious to me and I have access to them by my faith.

5. We Decree and Declare because of my Covenant with God, we will never live in a hopeless state in my relationship, in my life in Jesus' Name.

6. We Decree and Declare God had given us the Holy Spirit as a down payment for every promise written in His Word.

7. We Decree and Declare because of our Covenant with God, we have access to the Throne of God by the Blood of Jesus.

8. We Decree and Declare this Blessing is not just for me, but for everything that is connected to me.

9. We Decree and Declare because of the Covenant of God my children will always have a place of refuge in their hour of need.

10. We Decree and Declare my Covenant with God gives me confidence that whatever God has spoken about my marriage will come to pass without delay.

11. We Decree and Declare because of my Covenant with God I walk unhindered by Fear, Doubt and Disbelief.

12. We Decree and Declare our Covenant with God gives my marriage

and relationship access to supernatural favor, preferential treatment, opportunities granted, and abundance in every area of our life.

13. We Decree and Declare because of my Covenant with God our businesses are prospering and everything we touch multiplies.

14. We Decree and Declare my Covenant with God has eliminated lack, insufficiency, and every sign of poverty in my relationship, in my life, in my business, in my family, in my career, and in my ministry.

15. We Decree and Declare because my Covenant with God we are increasing more and more on a daily basis, even our children.

16. We Decree and Declare because in my Covenant with God we have dominion.

17. We Decree and Declare because of our Covenant with God we believe that we are created in God's image.

18. We Decree and Declare because my covenant with God gives us the authority to enforce God's will for our family and marriage.

19. We Decree and Declare because of our Covenant with God, no weapon formed against us shall Prosper and every tongue that is spoken against us we shall condemn in Jesus' name.

20. We Decree and Declare that today, not our will be done, but Your Will be done in every area of our lives.

21. We Decree and Declare our Covenant with God has established our relationship in the heavens and so shall it be in the earth.

22. We Decree and Declare because of our Covenant with God; we receive revelation and knowledge every day.

23. We Decree and Declare our Covenant with God is the source of our confidence, it is the source of our Faith, it is the source of our

expectation.

24. We Decree and Declare our Covenant gives an expectation that God will complete His Work through our relationship.

25. We Decree and Declare our Covenant with God makes all things possible for us.

—that at that time you were without Christ, being aliens from the commonwealth of Israel

and strangers from the covenants of promise,

having no hope and without God in the world.

Ephesians 2:12 (NKJV)

Reflections

Seventeen Day ~ Communication/Transparency

1. We Decree and Declare we will never let any corrupt communication proceed out of our mouth, only things that are edifying to those who hear it.

2. We Decree and Declare we operate in humility concerning one another and we renounce of every spirit of pride, arrogance, and selfishness.

3. We Decree and Declare we speak words of life, and we curse every idle and unproductive word.

4. We Decree and Declare our words are always seasoned with salt mixed with grace.

5. We Decree and Declare our mission is to build up our relationship and never pluck it down with our mouths.

6. We Decree and Declare in Christ we live, move, and have our being and will never step outside of His Grace.

7. We Decree and Declare we are committed to oneness with our Lord and Savior and becoming one with our spouse/partner.

8. We Decree and Declare; we are always open for correction and change and will never allow an offense to separate us.

9. We Decree and Declare our Love Walk is stable and is ever-increasing.

10. We Decree and Declare; we are always led by the Holy Spirit.

11. We Decree and Declare that our words will not return to us void and it will perform what we send it to do, in Jesus' Name.

12. We Decree and Declare we release the light of the gospel into every area of our lives in Jesus.

13. We Decree and Declare let there be light in our homes, relationships, finances, businesses, and ministry in Jesus' Name.

14. We Decree and Declare we release the Blessing of the Lord over every backbiter, persecutor, and person who despitefully uses us.

15. We Decree and Declare to let the communication of our Faith be effective as we acknowledge the Works of our Lord and Savior.

16. We Decree and Declare we acknowledge that every need we have is met in Jesus' Name.

17. We Decree and Declare we acknowledge that by the Stripes of Jesus, our marriage/relationship is healed in Jesus' Name.

18. We Decree and Declare; we acknowledge that the curse is broken off of our marriage/relationship.

19. We Decree and Declare we acknowledge that in our weakness, our marriage/relationship is made strong.

20. We Decree and Declare; we acknowledge our marriage/relationship is established by God, planted by God, and watered by God.

21. We Decree and Declare no weapon formed against us will prosper.

22. We Decree and Declare the Word of God has given us perfect eyesight.

23. We Decree and Declare; we walk by Faith; we walk in Love; we walk in Wisdom and we walk in the Light.

24. We Decree and Declare that there is more with us than against us.

25. We Decree and Declare our marriage/relationship Blessed and Highly Favored of the Lord.

"Let no corrupt word proceed out of your mouth, but what is good for necessary edification, that it may impart grace to the hearers."

Ephesians 4:29 (NKJV)

Reflections

Day Eighteen ~ Intimacy

1. We Decree and Declare we abide in Jesus and His Word and we only desire what God has for us.

2. We Decree and Declare our desires are sanctified and are not of the flesh.

3. We Decree and Declare in Jesus we live, we move and have our being.

4. We Decree and Declare daily we allow the Word to set boundaries for our marriage, family, career, finances, and ministry.

5. We Decree and Declare we agree with God on everything spoken words concerning our marriage and relationship and our steps are Ordered by the Lord.

6. We Decree and Declare our Intimacy produces answers, prayers that will not be hindered by any demonic foe.

7. We Decree and Declare our Intimacy with God produces supernatural favor in every area of our life.

8. We Decree and Declare because of our Intimacy with God, our love for God grows and with God's Love we are unstoppable.

9. We Decree and Declare because of the Love of God we will never experience failure.

10. We Decree and Declare because of our Intimacy with God we are always abounding with Grace and Peace.

11. We Decree and Declare our Intimacy brings us comfort and peace.

12. We Decree and Declare because of Intimacy with God our words command and strengthen our angelic support.

13. We Decree and Declare our Intimacy makes all things work out for our good.

14. We Decree and Declare because of our Intimacy with God, I am Known by Him, Loved by Him and Perfected by Him.

15. We Decree and Declare because of our Intimacy with God, He will complete the work He has started in our relationship.

16. We Decree and Declare we are One with God and the Holy Spirit as our guide, our teacher, and our help.

17. We Decree and Declare because of our Intimacy with God we can never be removed from His Love.

18. We Decree and Declare God's Love for us is eternal and everlasting.

19. We Decree and Declare that God's Love for us is not based on what we do for Him but who we are in Him.

20. We Decree and Declare God's Love empowers us to never allow for fear to overcome our relationship.

21. We Decree and Declare our Intimacy with God remove our fears, doubts, and anxiety.

22. We Decree and Declare because of our Intimacy with God we are new creatures and the <u>old man</u> is dead and has no power over our relationship.

23. We Decree and Declare because of Intimacy with God we resist the devil, and he always flees.

24. We Decree and Declare because of our Intimacy with God, the enemy is under our feet.

25. We Decree and Declare because of our Intimacy with God; we always win.

But he who is joined to the Lord is one spirit with Him.

1 Corinthians 6:17 (NKJV)

Reflections

Day Nineteen ~ Building a Solid Foundation

1. We Decree and Declare as the Word of God is settled in Heaven, so is our marriage/relationship.

2. We Decree and Declare the Word of God is a lamp upon our feet and a light to the darkness in every season of our lives.

3. We Decree and Declare we have hidden the Word of God in our hearts that we may NOT sin against God.

4. We Decree and Declare today we plant heaven in our marriage /relationship and sow Faith, Love, and Hope.

5. We Decree and Declare the Word of God is an anchor to our souls.

6. We Decree and Declare we receive the Mercy of God according to thy Word.

7. We Decree and Declare we are revived and quickened according to Thy Word.

8. We Decree and Declare the Word of God is the Voice of Jesus and another we will not follow.

9. We Decree and Declare the Word of God is the Truth of God, and I will never be deceived by the lie.

10. We Decree and Declare the Word of God empowers my faith for us to flow and live a supernatural lifestyle.

11. We Decree and Declare as Jesus is so I am.

12. We Decree and Declare we are a word sent from Heaven and we will perform that purpose God established before the foundation of the world.

13. We Decree and Declare we establish every area of our lives with the Word of God: Marriage, Family, Ministry, Finances, Career, and Business.

14. We stand in total agreement in what the Word of God says, and we live daily by the revelation of the Word.

15. We Decree and Declare the word gives us divine authority to establish God's Will in the earth.

16. We Decree and Declare the Word of God is the spirit of God that hovers over our lives.

17. We Decree and Declare the Word of God is my source of Wisdom, Knowledge and Understanding.

18. We Decree and Declare the Word of God will not return to me void, but it will accomplish everything I send it to do.

19. We Decree and Declare we release into our marriage/relationship strength, discipline, longsuffering, success, prosperity, and healing.

20. We Decree and Declare our response to the Word brings about our transformation by the Spirit of God.

21. We Decree and Declare our mind is renewed by the Word of God.

22. We Decree and Declare our hearts flow in the Word of God.

23. We Decree and Declare our bodies are healed by the Word of God.

24. We Decree and Declare our thoughts are screened by the Word of God.

25. We Decree and Declare the Word of God is the foundation of our entire house, and our house will never be condemned.

"Therefore, whoever hears these sayings of Mine, and does them, I will liken him to a wise man who built his house on the rock: and the rain descended, the floods came, and the winds blew and beat on that house; and it did not fall, for it was founded on the rock."

Mathew 7:24-25 (NKJV)

Reflections

Day Twenty ~ Loving Yourself

1. We Decree and Declare we are Fearfully and Wonderfully made by God and because of His love, we are confident in who we are.

2. We Decree and Declare that we are God's masterpiece and His workmanship.

3. We Decree and Declare we are the Beloved of God and His Love for us removes all my fears.

4. We Decree and Declare; we walk in the confidence of God's Love and our faith works through the Love of God.

5. We Decree and Declare we see ourselves the way God sees us, and we never think too highly of ourselves.

6. We Decree and Declare we believe everything God has said about us.

7. We Decree and Declare as Jesus is, so we are in this earth.

8. We Decree and Declare we are the salt of the earth.

9. We Decree and Declare we are the salt that sustains our relationship.

10. We Decree and Declare we are the Love of God that keeps everything together in our household.

11. We Decree and Declare we are God's Son and because of our Faith in Christ, God is well pleased with us.

12. We Decree and Declare we love ourselves with the same Love that God has for us.

13. We Decree and Declare we walk in the reality that we will never be condemned because of our Faith in Christ.

14. We Decree and Declare our Faith in Christ has made us precious to God.

15. We Decree and Declare because of God's Love for us we walk in the

authority of a Child of God.

16. We Decree and Declare because of God's Love for us; we walk in the confidence that my words can change my world according to my faith.

17. We Decree and Declare because of God's Love for us we have confidence in who we are in God.

18. We Decree and Declare we are God's representative on the earth.

19. We Decree and Declare we are co-labors with Christ Jesus.

20. We Decree and Declare what we say will come to pass just like that!

21. We Decree and Declare we call those things that be not, as though they were.

22. We Decree and Declare we love that God created us in His Image, and we Honor Him by acting just like He does.

23. We Decree and Declare we are built up in the Love of God and pride, low esteem will never be our portion.

24. We Decree and Declare that we will never give up on ourselves and our love for ourselves is Patient, Kind, Longsuffering and Resilient.

25. We Decree and Declare that our love for ourselves will never fail and will always grow under pressure.

I will praise You, for, I am fearfully *and* wonderfully made. Marvelous are Your works,

And *that* my soul knows very well.

Psalm 139:14 (NKJV)

Reflections

Day Twenty-One ~ Working Together

1. We Decree and Declare; we walk together in agreement with God's plans for our lives.

2. We Decree and Declare that we are always led by the Spirit of God in every decision we make.

3. We Decree and Declare we are one in Spirit, Soul, and Body.

4. We Decree and Declare we will not be separated by our differences.

5. We Decree and Declare our differences unify and complete us.

6. We Decree and Declare together that we have dominion; we are fruitful, we multiply, and we subdue every demonic hindrance.

7. We Decree and Declare we are the gap fillers to every need in our relationship.

8. We Decree and Declare our marriage/relationship is an assignment from God.

9. We Decree and Declare that our marriage/relationship flows with Unconditional Honor and Unconditional Love.

10. We Decree and Declare that our unity makes us unstoppable.

11. We Decree and Declare that the Word of God is our source for instruction.

12. We Decree and Declare that the Word of God is our strength in times of difficulty.

13. We Decree and Declare the Word of God is a lamp upon our feet.

14. We Decree and Declare we will support one another and do everything possible to help our spouse complete their divine assignment.

15. We Decree and Declare that we renounce selfishness, fear and every spirit that would hinder our successful union.

16. We Decree and Declare that we plead the Blood of Jesus over our union, and we have the ministry of reconciliation.

17. We Decree and Declare we look to always reconcile breaches in our relationship.

18. We Decree and Declare we never let the sun go down on our raft.

19. We Decree and Declare we will allow the Word of God to settle all our

conflicts.

20. We Decree and Declare we are right now in possession of everything pertaining to life and Godliness.

21. We Decree and Declare we are complete in Christ Jesus, nothing missing, nothing broken.

22. We Decree and Declare our expectation is of God.

23. We Decree and Declare that we expect to win in every area of our lives.

24. We Decree and Declare Goodness and Mercy will follow us all the days of our lives.

25. We Decree and Declare our relationship is planted by rivers of water, and we produce fruit in every season.

"Again I say to you that if two of you agree on earth concerning anything that they ask, it will be done for them by My Father in heaven."

Matthew 18:19 (NKJV)

Reflections

Day Twenty-Two ~ Purpose

1. Our marriage is an Assignment of God, and He watches over it and it will perform that which it was sent to do in the earth.

2. Our marriage reflects the Image of God, and through our marriage, our family will see what God looks like.

3. Our marriage is a reflection of the Unity of God.

4. Our marriage is the foundation of our entire family and a light that sits on a hill and everyone sees.

5. Our marriage reflects the Love of God on the earth.

6. Our marriage will NEVER fail but will ALWAYS grow in difficult times.

7. In our marriage, our love for one another is not based on our emotions but will always decide to Love.

8. In our marriage, the Grace of God abounds, even as sin abounds giving Glory to God.

9. Our marriage is the vehicle that God uses to transform our very soul.

10. In our marriage, we Honor God by honoring His Covenant.

11. In our marriage, God will make a way for when we are tempted outside His will for our lives.

12. Our marriage is a reflection of the Fear of God.

13. Our marriage walks in the Wisdom of God.

14. Because of the Fear of God, our marriage will experience long life, perpetual favor, supernatural increase, and preferred treatment by the Grace of God.

15. Our marriage is a picture of the Gospel of our Lord Jesus Christ.

16. Our marriage is a seed from Heaven that will grow and produce fruit for all that need it.

17. Our marriage is a picture of what Dominion Loves.

18. Our marriage is a picture of Sacrifice, Honor, Love, and Unity.

19. Our marriage is an unstoppable force in the earth and will not be hindered

by any demonic foe.

20. Because of our union with God, our spiritual and natural children are Blessed and Favored by God.

21. Because of our union with God, our children will always have a place of refuge in their times of trouble.

22. Because of our union with God, our children will receive double of what is on our lives.

23. We will receive Favor from God and man and every good thing that we put their hands too will be Blessed.

24. In our marriage, the Blessings of the Lord will overtake us adding no sorrow.

25. Our marriage is one with our Father in Heaven in Jesus' Name.

"For we are His workmanship, created in Christ Jesus for good works, which God prepared beforehand that we should walk in them."

Ephesians 2:10 (NKJV)

Reflections

Day Twenty-Three ~ Vision

1. We Decree and Declare today we walk in the Vision of God for our lives.

2. We Decree and Declare we walk by faith and not by sight.

3. We Decree and Declare our lives are united with the Word of God and the Wisdom of God rest on our lips.

4. We Decree and Declare the Word of God provides insight into the Vision of God.

5. We Decree and Declare because of the Vision of God, our marriage /relationship will accelerate through the Revelation of God.

6. We Decree and Declare we believe; therefore, we speak the Vision of God into our marriage/relationship.

7. We Decree and Declare the Word of God in our vision for our relationship, therefore, we release by faith: Abundance, Healing, Prosperity, and Deliverance.

8. We Decree and Declare we are always guided by wisdom and in times of difficulty, we search for it.

9. We Decree and Declare we come against spiritual blindness, and we command our eyes to open now in the Name of Jesus.

10. We Decree and Declare we were created in the image of God, so see in the natural and the spiritual realm.

11. We Decree and Declare we are sensitive to the moving of the Holy Spirit and when God moves, we move.

12. We Decree and Declare we walk in an understanding that every need we have, a supply has already been given.

13. We Decree and Declare we see every circumstance, situation, and

contradiction through the Word of God.

14. We Decree and Declare we see the Word of God as my answer for every problem we face.

15. We Decree and Declare the Word of God helps me see the end from the beginning.

16. We Decree and Declare the Word of God helps me see that I have already won.

17. We Decree and Declare the Word of God helps me see that I am peace.

18. We Decree and Declare the Word of God helps me see all things are possible with God.

19. We Decree and Declare because of the Word we will always see ourselves coming out of what appears to be hopeless situations.

20. We Decree and Declare because of the Word of God we are light in dark places.

21. We Decree and Declare as I walk in purity, I will always see God working on my behalf.

22. We Decree and Declare, today I release my faith to have daily encounters with God.

23. We Decree and Declare our faith is the vehicle that God uses to introduce Himself to us.

24. We Decree and Declare as I see Him, I will become just like Him.

25. We Decree and Declare that we will always taste and see the goodness working in our life.

"But he who hates his brother is in darkness and walks in darkness,

and does not know where he is going, because the darkness has blinded his eyes."

1 Joh 2:11 (NKJV)

Reflections

Day Twenty-Four – Consistency

1. We Decree and Declare we live, move, and have our being in God.

2. We Decree and Declare we walk in the Light of God, and we have no fellowship with darkness.

3. We Decree and Declare we walk in the Love of God, and we have no fellowship with selfishness.

4. We Decree and Declare; we walk in the Wisdom of God, and we have no connection with foolishness.

5. We Decree and Declare we walk in the Spirit and will not fulfill the lust of the flesh.

6. We Decree and Declare we walk by Faith, and we will not allow circumstances, situations, or contradictions to set the agenda in our relationship/marriage.

7. We Decree and Declare; we live by every word that proceeds out of the Mouth of God.

8. We Decree and Declare we are Consistently Casting Down every thought and contradiction that comes against our Dreams, our Purpose, our Finances, our Health, our Marriage, and our Family in Jesus' Name.

9. We Decree and Declare we make a commitment today to align our hearts with the Heart of God.

10. We Decree and Declare; we speak to our soul's Strength, Stability, and Servanthood in Jesus' Name.

11. We Decree and Declare that we have established another level of Order and Honor in all that we do.

12. We Decree and Declare that we are Consistently Committed to Loving, Honoring, Enduring, and Persevering in the Things of God.

13. We Decree and Declare we are Consistently Resisting every temptation that would frustrate and derail the Plan of God for our relationship, marriage, and

family.

14. We Decree and Declare that we Consistently Plant the heavens into our relationship.

15. We Decree and Declare that we Consistently Plead the Blood of Jesus in every area of our life.

16. We Decree and Declare we are Consistently Praying Thy will be done, Thy kingdom come in Jesus' Name NOW!

17. We Decree and Declare we are Consistently Speaking the truth over every lie spoken against our relationship/marriage.

18. We Decree and Declare we Consistently Believe all things are possible with God.

19. We Decree and Declare that we Consistently Believe that all things will work out for our good.

20. We Decree and Declare we always win in every area of our life.

21. We Decree and Declare that we consistently will always believe that we will never fail at becoming One with God.

22. We Decree and Declare that we Consistently Believe that Love covers a multitude of sins.

23. We Decree and Declare we Consistently Believe that our marriage/ relationship will fulfill the purpose that God established in Heaven.

24. We Decree and Declare; we consistently believe that Life and Death are in the power of the tongue, and we release the Life of God consistently in our relationship.

25. We Decree and Declare we consistently call those things that be not, as though they were in Jesus' Name.

Then Jesus said to those Jews who believed Him, "If you abide in My word, you are My disciples indeed. And you shall know the truth, and the truth shall make you free."

John 8:31-32

Reflections

Day Twenty-Five ~ Agreement

1. We Decree and Declare we are one in Body, Soul, and Spirit.

2. We Decree and Declare that our lives are knitted together by the Bond of Love and our Faith in Christ Jesus.

3. We Decree and Declare because of our relationship with Christ Jesus; we are one with God, and the Holy Spirit dwells within us.

4. We Decree and Declare we are unified by the Spirit of God, sanctified by the Word of God and strengthened by the Revelation of God.

5. We Decree and Declare our agreement with God gives us access to every Promise of Christ Jesus.

6. We Decree and Declare that we touch and agreement on the promise of Health, Wealth, Prosperity, and Deliverance in Jesus' Name.

7. We Decree and Declare that we stand in agreement for the Salvation of all family members and friends.

8. We Decree and Declare we command their Spiritual Eyes to be open and for them to be sanctified by the truth.

9. We Decree and Declare we stand in agreement that NO weapon formed against our marriage/relationship, Family, Ministry, and Business shall prosper.

10. We Decree and Declare as it is in Heaven, so shall it be in our relationship.

11. We Decree and Declare Thy kingdom come, God will be done today and forever in our relationship.

12. We Decree and Declare we are in agreement that Miracles, Signs and Wonders follow us the days of our lives because of our Faith in God.

13. We Decree and Declare we are in agreement that we live a supernatural lifestyle, and we receive supernatural results.

14. We agree that we will always increase more and more, even our children.

15. We Decree and Declare the Blessing of the Lord will overtake us in every area of our lives.

16. We Decree and Declare the Blessing of the Lord has made us rich with no sorrow.

17. We Decree and Declare we grow in Favor with God and man.

18. We Decree and Declare; we commit our ways to the Lord and our thoughts are established.

19. We Decree and Declare, we believe; therefore, we speak the end from the beginning.

20. We bind every demonic attack that has come against our Marriage, Family, Business, Career, and Ministry.

21. We Decree and Declare we loose the Love of God in our lives and reject every setback, difficulty, and mediocre results.

22. We Decree and Declare we agree that the Love of God voids all failure in our lives.

23. We Decree and Declare we agree that the Power of the Holy Spirit will resurrect us from every dead situation, circumstance, or contradiction in our marriage.

24. We Decree and Declare we command our Ministering to be released now to bring to best every word spoken in this injunction in Jesus' Name.

Can two walk together, unless they are agreed?

Amos 3:3 (NKJV)

Reflections

Day Twenty-Six ~ Focus

1. As we look to the hills from which comes our help, our help comes from the Lord.

2. We Focus our minds and our spirit on the finished Works of Christ.

3. As we Focus on Christ and His Word, our marriage/relationship is being transformed by His Spirit.

4. We set our hearts and minds on the things that are above.

5. Our Focus will not be interrupted by depressive thoughts, fear, unbelief, and anxiety.

6. As we Focus on Christ, we become just like Him.

7. As He is, so are we in this Word.

8. Because of our Focus, our minds are renewed daily by the Word of God.

9. Our Focus empowers our diligence, and our diligence empowers our plans.

10. Our Faith is empowered by our Focus, and we dominate all negative circumstances, situations, and contradictions.

11. Because of our Focus, we refused to settle for anything less than God's best for our Marriage, Family, Career, Finance, and Ministry.

12. Because of our Focus, we refused to consider anything God did not say.

13. Because of our Focus on the Promises of God we will not waver or drawback.

14. Because of our Focus, our Faith is strengthened, giving Glory to God.

15. Our Focus is intensifying every day, and the Power of God is increasing at my level of Focus.

16. Our Focus, mixed with our Faith produces supernatural results.

17. Whatever I Focus on, I will become.

18. Today we Focus on the result: Victory, Peace, Love, and the Joy of the Lord.

19. Whatever we Focus on, we draw into our lives.

20. We draw into our lives every resource necessary to complete our Divine Assignment.

21. Because of our Focus, opportunities come to us daily, Favor is granted to us daily, Good and Mercy follow us daily.

22. Because of our Focus, we will not be tempted by the counterfeits sent by the enemy.

23. Because of our Focus we decern good from evil.

24. We Focus on walking in the Wisdom of God, and we reject compromising word sent by the enemy.

25. Our Focus has made us an overcomer by the Blood of the Lamb and the Word of our Testimony.

"I will lift up my eyes to the hill, from whence comes my help?

My help comes from the Lord, Who made heaven and earth."

Psalms 121:1-3

Reflections

Day Twenty-Seven ~ Prosperity

1. We Decree and Declare, we walk in Divine Health and Prosper even as our soul Prospers.

2. We Decree and Declare today that we increase more and more, even our children.

3. We Decree and Declare we take possession of everything pertaining to Life and Godliness.

4. We Decree and Declare that Jesus's death and resurrection have given us access to the Abundant Life.

5. We Decree and Declare daily, we grow in the Wisdom of God, and we increase in Favor with God and man.

6. We Decree and Declare the Blessing of the Lord has made us rich in every area of our lives.

7. We Decree and Declare I am amply supplied by God for every good endeavor.

8. We Decree and Declare we don't Walk in the Fear of Lack because every need I have is supplied by God.

9. We Decree and Declare that the Blood of Jesus has broken the limitations off our marriage/relationship, and there is nothing that we can't accomplish together.

10. We Decree and Declare together that we have dominion over the Works of God's hands, and we are fruitful and we multiply everything we touch in Jesus' Name.

11. We Decree and Declare it is God's will for us to Prosper and be in good health.

12. We Decree and Declare our increase is of God and it gives God Glory when we increase.

13. We Decree and Declare as we plant the heavens, God will receive an increase on every seed sown.

14. We Decree and Declare we walk in the Hundredfold Blessing.

15. We Decree and Declare we will receive Hundredfold Blessing because we are sold out to God.

16. We Decree and Declare as we sow by the spirit, we will receive a harvest in that same year.

17. We Decree and Declare this is our season of acceleration; what took years will now take months, what took months will now take weeks, what took weeks will now take days, and what took days will now take hours in Jesus' Name.

18. We Decree and Declare we will never be broke another day in our life.

19. We Decree and Declare we believe; therefore, we speak that God is raising up somebody somewhere to be a Blessing in my life and ministry.

20. We Decree and Declare our financial Boaz we see ourselves working in God's field and releasing Blessings in our life.

21. We Decree and Declare that every need we have is met in Jesus.

22. We Decree and Declare the wealth of the wicked is released into our hands now in Jesus' Name.

23. We Decree and Declare that we command the wicked to release into our lives riches, wealth, and every valuable material goods.

24. We Decree and Declare our Faith is made effective by thanking God in advance before any physical manifestation.

25. We Decree and Declare we Thank You, Lord, for Your love, which has anticipated my every need.

...Beloved, I pray that you may prosper in all things

and be in health just as your soul prospers.

3 John 2 (NKJV)

Reflections

Day Twenty-Eight ~ Obedience

1. We Decree and Declare we are Willing and Obedient, and we take possession of the good of the land.

2. We Decree and Declare our Obedience releases the Blessing into our lives.

3. We Decree and Declare because of our Obedience angels are Strengthened and Empowered at the sound of our voice.

4. We Decree and Declare our Obedience connects to the Blessing.

5. We Decree and Declare our Obedience positions us to receive the Blessing.

6. We Decree and Declare that our Faith in Christ has made us the seed of Abraham.

7. We Decree and Declare because of our Obedience, we are the Righteousness of God in Christ Jesus.

8. We Decree and Declare that because of our Obedience, there will always be a ram in the bush.

9. We Decree and Declare our Obedience enables us to see what God has given us.

10. We Decree and Declare our Obedience positions our prayers as a memorial to God.

11. We Decree and Declare our Obedience gives us access to Supernatural Favor, Preferential Treatment, Petitions granted and Material wealth.

12. We Decree and Declare that the gold and the silver are ours and every necessary resource to fulfill our assignment on the earth.

13. We Decree and Declare that our Obedience is better than our sacrifice.

14. We Decree and Declare we Walk in the Spirit, and we will not fulfill our fleshly desires.

15. We Decree and Declare that we delight ourselves in the Lord, and always gives us the desires of hearts.

16. We Decree and Declare because we delight ourselves in the Lord; God does Exceedingly and Abundantly above all we ever ask or think.

17. We Decree and Declare because of our Obedience, we live a life free from guilt, and our Faith operates at the great Faith level.

18. We Decree and Declare because of our Obedience, we are empowered by the Grace.

19. We Decree and Declare our Obedience gives us access to God's Power and Authority.

20. We Decree and Declare because of our Obedience, our confidence grows.

21. We Decree and Declare because of our Obedience, we are confident that our Prayers are heard by God.

22. We Decree and Declare our obedience to God is our motivation to always Forgive, always Love, and always Honor our spouse.

23. We Decree and Declare our Obedience gives of strength to stand during difficult times in our marriage.

24. We Decree and Declare because of our Obedience, we trust God, and we receive the reward of happiness.

25. We Decree and Declare our Obedience connects us to the Power of the Blood and the Blood of Jesus cleanses our bloodline, and the curse is broken off our Family, Career, Finances, and Ministry in Jesus' Name.

"If you are willing and obedient, You shall eat the good of the land; But if you refuse and rebel, You shall be devoured by the sword,"

For the mouth of the Lord has spoken."

Isaiah 1:19-20

Reflections

Day Twenty-Nine ~ Submission

1. We Decree and Declare Thy kingdom come Thy will be done, as it is in Heaven, so it shall be in our marriage.

2. We Decree and Declare we superimpose Your Will over the will of Satan in our marriage.

3. We Decree and Declare we crucify our flesh and surrender our will, not our will, but Your will be done in Jesus' Name.

4. We Decree and Declare we realigned our values to match Your values.

5. We Decree and Declare we Submit our Gifts, Talents, and Abilities for the edifying of our relationship.

6. We submit our lives to the Bond of Love and Unconditional Honor toward one another.

7. We Decree and Declare we Humbly Submit to Your way of Thinking, Acting, and Believing towards one another in Jesus' Name.

8. We Decree and Declare we Submit our tongue to the move of the Holy Spirit, and we will not release any unproductive word into our relationship.

9. We Submit and make a Commitment to always renew our minds to prove the Will of God in our marriage.

10. We Decree and Declare that we Submit to protect our union and we will not allow outside influences above the Word of God.

11. We Decree and Declare that we Submit and are Committed to presenting the God's Image to our Family, Friends, and Community.

12. We Decree and Declare we Submit to walking by Faith in Love concerning our marriage.

13. We submit to always believing for God's best for another.

14. We Decree and Declare we submit to never quitting on ourselves and our spouse.

15. We Decree and Declare we submit to resisting the enemies' attacks and

believing that God will make a way for our escape.

16. We Decree and Declare that we submit to always believing in one another and we will never tear down but always build each other up.

17. We Decree and Declare we submit to the understanding that my spouse is my curricular development.

18. We Decree and Declare; we submit to building our house by the Word of God.

19. We Decree and Declare we submit, allowing the Holy Spirit to correct our behavior and lack of understanding concerning the things of God.

20. We Decree and Declare; we submit to not receiving ungodly counsel nor standing or walking with people who don't have the heart of God.

21. We Decree and Declare we submit to being a tree planted by rivers of water, producing fruit in every season.

22. We Decree and Declare that we submit to Eden's mandate given by God to be fruitful, multiply and subdue every adversary that comes against our relationship.

23. We Decree and Declare that we submit to producing the Fruit of Love, Joy, Peace, Longsuffering, Patience, Brotherly Kindness, Faithfulness, Goodness, and Self-Control.

24. We Decree and Declare we Submit, taking Dominion over all the works of God's hands.

25. We Decree and Declare, we Submit and commit to always growing my personal relationship with the Lord.

"…giving thanks always for all things to God the Father in the name of our Lord Jesus Christ, submitting to one another in the fear of God."

Ephesians 5:20-21 (NKJV)

Reflections

Day Thirty – Gratitude

1. We Decree and Declare we Thank You, Lord, that our Faith is made effective by acknowledging the finished works of Christ.

2. We Decree and Declare that we Thank You, Lord, for making every provision for us before the foundation of the world.

3. We Decree and Declare we Thank You, Lord, that the Blood of Jesus has broken every curse off our lives.

4. We Decree and Declare we Thank You, Lord, that because of the Blood of Jesus, we can come boldly to the Throne of Grace in our time of need.

5. We Decree and Declare we Thank You, Lord, that the Blood has given us the confidence to receive Your Love.

6. We Decree and Declare we Thank You, Lord, and remain Grateful for all the promises.

7. We Decree and Declare that we Thank You, Lord, for saying yes to all of our needs.

8. We Decree and Declare that we Thank You, Lord, for always providing seed for the Sower.

9. We Decree and Declare we Thank You, Lord, for Your supernatural manifestation concerning our provision.

10. We Decree and Declare we Thank You, Lord, for setting our expectations according to Your Word; our expectation is from You.

11. We Decree and Declare we Thank You, Lord, that we are recipients of Your covenant kindness.

12. We Decree and Declare we Thank You, Lord, for creating us in Your Image, and we are Your workmanship.

13. We Decree and Declare we Thank You, Lord, that because of our Faith in Christ Jesus, we have been made righteous.

14. We Decree and Declare we Thank You, Lord, that because we have been made right, the Blessing has been poured on our heads.

15. We Decree and Declare that we Thank You, Lord, for crowning us with Your Glory and Honor.

16. We Decree and Declare we Thank You, Lord, for being a God of many chances.

17. We Decree and Declare that we Thank You, Lord, for being mindful that we are just dust.

18. We Decree and Declare we Thank You, Lord, for our Salvation: We are free from Sickness, Poverty, and Death in Jesus' Name.

19. We Decree and Declare that we Thank You, Lord, for going ahead of us, making the crooked place straight and getting behind us, protecting us from our past.

20. We Decree and Declare we Thank You, Lord, for an endless supply of Your goodness and mercy.

21. We Decree and Declare that we Thank You, Lord, for being the good Shepherd and You're the only voice we will follow.

22. We Decree and Declare that we Thank You, Lord, for being our supply for every need.

23. We Decree and Declare we Thank You, Lord, that Jesus' Victory over Satan is our victory.

24. We Decree and Declare we Thank You, Lord, that because of Jesus, we always will in every area of our lives.

25. We Thank You, Lord, that Jesus is the source of our confidence, and His Word is the source of my Faith.

"…in everything give thanks; for this is the will of God in Christ Jesus for you." 1 Thessalonians 5:18 (NKJV)

Reflections

Day Thirty-One ~ Prayer

1. We Decree and Declare in the Name of Jesus, and we Pray that every promise spoken concerning us will come to pass.

2. We Decree and Declare we Pray, Oh God, that we would increase even more and more.

3. We Decree and Declare that we Thank You, Lord, that Jesus is the source of our confidence in Your Word.

4. We Decree and Declare this is the confidence that we have that if we Pray according to Your Word, we know that You always hear us and we have our petitions granted in Jesus' Name.

5. We Decree and Declare that our Father in Heaven releases unto us every necessary resource for us to complete our divine assignment.

6. We Decree and Declare Father anoint our lips of clay, and let none of our words hit the ground.

7. We Decree and Declare that none of our words will return void, but they will accomplish what we sent them to perform.

8. We Decree and Declare that we walk in divine healing and sickness and disease are far from us.

9. We Decree and Declare we are virus-free; if any virus touches our body, it will instantly die.

10. We Decree and Declare, we plead the Blood of Jesus over our entire household, and we are protected from the curse of the law.

11. We Decree and Declare we are overcomers by the Blood of the Lamb and the word of our testimony.

10.	We Decree and Declare in times of trouble; we call You, and You answer us speedily.

11.	We Decree and Declare we call those things that be not as though they were, and our atmosphere is set for supernatural growth.

12.	We Decree and Declare that we would have all sufficiency in all things.

13.	We Decree and Declare that our children will have a place of refuge because we Fear the Lord.

14.	We Decree and Declare Father in Heaven we Pray that you would bring an increase of a hundredfold on every seed sown in Faith.

15.	We Decree and Declare, Father, we ask that You vindicate us from everything that our adversary has caused, directly and indirectly.

16.	We Decree and Declare we turn from our wickedness and repent from our sins.

17.	We Decree and Declare we ask You, Oh God, to heal our land and restore everything the cankerworm ate up.

18.	We Decree and Declare as from me and my house, we will serve the Lord.

19.	We Decree and Declare open the blinded eyes of our loved ones, family, and friends. That they may see the Light of the Gospel.

20.	We Decree and Declare, sanctify them by the truth and enlighten their eyes of their understanding.

21.	We Decree and Declare, Father, we ask for Your wisdom to make the right decisions.

22.	We Decree and Declare Father, we ask for a greater understanding of who You are in our lives.

23.   We Decree and Declare, Father, we ask that You give us a greater anointing to raise the dead, heal the sick, and cast our demons.

25.   We Decree and Declare, Father, we ask that You stretch forth Your hand today and assist us in accomplishing everything spoken in this prayer.

26.   Father, we ask that You stretch forth Your hand today and assist us to accomplish everything spoken in this prayer.

"I thank God, whom I serve with a pure conscience, as my forefathers did, as without ceasing I remember you in my prayers night and day."

2 Timothy 1:3 (NKJV)

Reflections

ABOUT THE AUTHORS

The Relationship Drs./Drs. Timothy & Monique Johns

The Relationship Dr's Tim and Monique Johns have been married for 27 years. Their transparent approach to providing practical solutions to everyday relationships challenge has inspired thousands. They believe that to be Married for Life (M4Life), both partners must die to their selfish nature. Putting to death selfishness is the number one key to having a successful relationship.

Through their journey together, they have purposely remained friends. Their friendship has produced flexibility and cohesiveness, which has been the other source of their longevity. Tim & Monique's triangle of LOVE is supported by God being their ex-factor.

They are also the founders of Heaven's Gate Ministries, The Dream Leadership Institute, A Helping Hand, Living Outside the Walls, and several businesses. Their Relationship Drs' broadcast can be viewed weekly on all social media platforms. They are the proud parents of Gabriella, Timothy II, Vincenzia, and Giovanna.

Their scriptural focus: Hebrew 13:5 "For he said himself, I would never leave you or forsake you." M4Life!